Digby
and
the Big
Flood

by
Alan Aburrow-Newman

Illustrated by
Gill Guile

Brimax · Newmarket · England

Digby was digging a trench along the edge of the road by the river.
It had been raining hard and Big Bill had to get a pump to suck the
water out of the trench. Digby liked working with the pump - it made
a lovely slurping noise and poured muddy water over the road.

Digby noticed there was more and more water in the trench. The pump
couldn't suck the water out fast enough.
"What's going on?" cried Digby. "We need another pump."
"I don't think it would help if we had ten pumps," said Big Bill. "Look! The
river has burst its banks - the whole town will be flooded soon!"

Digby looked along the road that ran into town. The streets and gardens were disappearing under water.
"Come on, Big Bill," said Digby. "We must see if we can help!"

As they drove along the main street and into the middle of town, Digby and Big Bill saw people leaning out of windows, calling for help.
"The town is completely flooded," called Lenny the baker.
"And the telephones and electricity are cut off," said Maggie from the pizza house.

"We can't get any help!"
Just then, Digby saw Jimmy Seed's farm trailer in an alley.
"Don't worry, I have an idea," he said. "Let's hitch up that trailer, Big Bill,
then we can pick up all the stranded people."

With the trailer behind him, Digby drove slowly through the flooded streets. He stopped under windows so people could climb down into the trailer. At some houses, the windows were so high, Digby used his back arm like a slide so people could slide down to the trailer.

Mrs McKenzie at the pet store had her two goats, Clarence and Susan with her. They were bleating for help. Clarence was so nervous, he was eating a tablecloth.

"How can we all get down?" called Mrs McKenzie to Digby.
"Climb into my back bucket and I will lift you down into the trailer."
"But we can't all get into that little bucket," said Mrs McKenzie.
"There's Clarence, Susan and me, three parrots in cages, two rabbits,
four kittens and a puppy!"

"You will have to take it in turns," said Digby. "Put all the animals in first."

Mrs McKenzie persuaded the two greedy goats to hop from the window by tossing a tasty-looking potted plant into the bucket. Then Mrs McKenzie carefully lifted the small animals and the parrots into Digby's bucket. Once the animals were safe, it was Mrs McKenzie's turn to ride in Digby's bucket. At last Digby called, "Hold on tight!" And with the trailer loaded with people and animals, he set off through the swirling water.

As they drove through the flooded town, Digby saw Pete the taxi driver. He seemed to be sitting *on* the water.

"That's very clever of you," called Digby. "You must be a very floaty sort of person to be able to sit *on* the water!"

"I'm not sitting on the water," replied Pete. "I'm sitting on the roof of my taxi! Have you any room for me in your trailer?"

"I'm sure we have space for a floaty taxi driver," said Digby with a smile.

Everyone squeezed up a little more to make room for Pete. Then off they went again, heading out of town towards the hills.

They were just passing the 'Supa Slick Oil Company' when Lenny the baker called out, "You had better get a move on, Digby. The water is coming into the trailer."

"I can't go any faster," puffed Digby. "It's really hard work pulling such a heavy trailer through this deep water."

"We need a boat," said Big Bill.

"Or we could be a boat," said Digby, as he watched a big, red oil barrel float past. Then he noticed more empty barrels bobbing around in the oil company yard. Digby had another idea.

"Come on, Big Bill," he said. "We need those oil barrels tied to me and the trailer!"

Big Bill climbed down into the water and caught hold of a barrel. He tied it tightly to Digby's front bucket with rope. Then helped by Lenny and Pete, Big Bill surrounded Digby with empty barrels. Then they collected more barrels and tied them to the trailer.

"We may be the strangest boat ever seen," said Digby, "but at least we should float if the water gets any deeper."

Digby and the trailer headed towards the bridge. Suddenly Digby stopped. He could see green hills and fields just across the river. "The bridge is under water," he said. "It might be unsafe to cross."

"We will have to try and drive over the bridge to check that it is safe,"
said Big Bill. "It might even be washed away in the middle."
They left the trailer tied to a tree so that it didn't float away. Then Digby
and Big Bill drove slowly across the bridge.

"I hope these oil barrel floats work," said Digby.
Suddenly, Digby's big front wheels tipped off the edge of the broken bridge.
"Oh, no!" cried Digby. "Hold on, Big Bill!" and with a huge splash they disappeared under the water like a diving whale. Then Digby bounced off the river bed and began to float back to the surface! Whoosh! He burst back into rainy sunshine.

Everyone on the trailer cheered as Digby bobbed along.

"These barrels may not be the best-looking water wings, but they certainly work," said Big Bill in relief, emptying water from his boots. "Oh, I knew they would," said Digby, who was secretly more relieved than Big Bill. "My ideas always work."

Spinning his rear wheels like a paddle steamer and using his back
bucket as a rudder, Digby headed back to the trailer.
"Full steam ahead, Captain!" he called happily.
Digby towed everyone safely across the river.
"Who needs bridges!" he said cheerfully as he pulled his friends onto
dry land.